D0310265

Digger Don

by Elizabeth Dale

Illustrated by Paul Dronsfield

W
FRANKLIN WATTS
LONDON • SYDNEY

Notes on the series

TIDDLERS are structured to provide support for children who are starting to read on their own. The stories may also be used for sharing with children.

Starting to read alone can be daunting. **TIDDLERS** help by listing the words in the book for a check before reading, and by providing visual support and repeating words and phrases. These books will both develop confidence and encourage reading and rereading for pleasure.

If you are reading this book with a child, here are a few suggestions:

1. Make reading fun! Choose a time to read when you and the child are relaxed and have time to share the story.
2. Talk about the story before you start reading. Look at the cover and the blurb. What might the story be about? Why might the child like it?
3. Look also at the list of words below - can the child tackle most of the words?
4. Encourage the child to retell the story, using the jumbled picture puzzle.
5. Give praise! Remember that small mistakes need not always be corrected.

Here is a list of the words in this story.

Common words:

a	is	the
and	next	there
are	not	to
can	stop	trees
day	stops	up
he	suddenly	

Other words:

dig	Don	flash
digs	dry	starts
diggers	getting	wet
digging	fences	

There is a flash!

4

Suddenly, Don
starts to dig.

7

And dig ...

And dig!

11

He digs up trees ...

... and fences.

He can not stop!

17

The next day, the diggers are dry.

19

And Don stops digging!

21

Puzzle Time

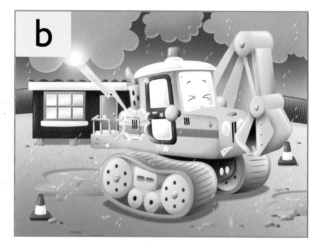

Can you find these
pictures in the story?

Which pages are the pictures from?

Turn over for answers!

Answers

The pictures come from these pages:

a. pages 18–19

b. pages 4–5

c. pages 20–21

d. pages 10–11

First published in 2014 by
Franklin Watts
338 Euston Road
London
NW1 3BH

Franklin Watts Australia
Level 17/207 Kent Street
Sydney
NSW 2000

Text © Elizabeth Dale 2014
Illustration © Paul Dronsfield 2014
The rights of Elizabeth Dale to be
identified as the author and Paul Dronsfield
as the illustrator of this Work have been
asserted in accordance with the Copyright,
Designs and Patents Act, 1988.

A CIP catalogue record for this book is
available from the British Library.

ISBN 978 1 4451 3262 4 (hbk)
ISBN 978 1 4451 3264 8 (pbk)
ISBN 978 1 4451 3261 7 (ebook)
ISBN 978 1 4451 3263 1 (library ebook)

Series Editor: Jackie Hamley
Editor: Melanie Palmer
Series Advisor: Catherine Glavina
Series Designer: Peter Scoulding

Printed in China

Franklin Watts is a divi ion of Hachette Children's Books,
an Hachette UK co1 ipany. www.hachette.co.uk